Fizzy and the Party

SARAH CROSSAN

ILLUSTRATED BY NICOLA COLTON

BLOOMSBURY EDUCATION

BLOOMSBURY EDUCATION

Bloomsbury Publishing Plc

50 Bedford Square, London, WC1B 3DP, UK

29 Earlsfort Terrace, Dublin 2, Ireland

BLOOMSBURY, BLOOMSBURY EDUCATION and the Diana logo
are trademarks of Bloomsbury Publishing Plc

First published in Great Britain in 2021 by Bloomsbury Publishing Plc

A catalogue record for this book is available from the British Library

ISBN: PB: 978-1-4729-7098-5; ePDF: 978-1-4729-7095-4; ePub: 978-1-4729-7094-7;
enhanced ePub: 978-1-4729-7097-8

2 4 6 8 10 9 7 5 3 1

Printed and bound in China by Leo Paper Products, Heshan, Guangdong

All papers used by Bloomsbury Publishing Plc are natural, recyclable products from wood
grown in well managed forests and other sources. The manufacturing processes conform to
the environmental regulations of the country of origin

To find out more about our authors and books visit www.bloomsbury.com
and sign up for our newsletters

Chapter One

For supper, Mum gave Fizzy a hot piece of toast and a cup of milk. She said, "Eat up quickly. It's getting late." Fizzy ignored Mum and opened her dressing up box.

In the box, along with masks, tutus and swords, were a few stray, dusty cola bottles so Fizzy popped them into her mouth. She chewed as she found a glittery party dress and held it up against her.

"Too small for me," she said and, grinning at her dog Bandit, grabbed him and popped his head through the hole in the dress. "Oh, you look fancy," she said. "Where are you off to at this time of night?"
Bandit stared up at her, unimpressed.

"Fizzy, please eat up," Mum said.
"And I don't think it's a good idea
to begin dressing up games this
late. How about you play with
Bandit tomorrow?"
"But it's not a game," Fizzy said.
"We're going to a party."
"What party?" Mum asked.

"Mrs Crumbleboom told me she was having a party tonight and as I'm her very best friend, I think it's rude not to show up. She said there would be actual real-life popping fireworks and I just *love* fireworks, you know I do!"

Mum shook her head. "You have school tomorrow. Come on now. Supper time."

Grumpily, Fizzy sat at the table and ate her toast. "Are you *sure* it's bedtime?" she asked.

Mum nodded. "I'm very sure."

Chapter Two

After her bath, Fizzy ran into her bedroom and shut the door. "I'll put on my pyjamas myself!" she shouted. "You can empty the bath or fill the dishwasher or feed Bandit. He looks quite hungry."

Bandit whined. He did look a bit hungry.

"Fine," Mum said. "But I'll be up in
three minutes to read you a story.
Be as quick as you can!"

Fizzy giggled and two minutes later appeared in the kitchen wearing a tiara, light-up fairy wings, and lots of Mum's make-up. Then she spotted a bottle with flowers on the side and, mistaking it for perfume, sprayed it on her wrists.

"Fizzy!" Mum cried out. "That's
furniture polish!"

"Is it?" Fizzy twirled on the spot. "But
I smell gorgeous. Like a queen."

"A queen who should be in bed."

"Queens don't have bed times. They
are in charge," Fizzy said.

"Now, take me to the party next door.
Immediately. You are, after all, my
royal servant."
Mum squinted. "Upstairs right now,
Your Highness."

Fizzy's face got all
scrunched up, and
she was just about to
say something that
might have got her into
trouble, when, luckily,
the back door swung
open.
"Hello! Anyone at
home?" It was Mrs
Crumbleboom, their
neighbour.

"Come in!" Mum said. Mrs Crumbleboom looked down at Bandit, then over at Fizzy, and clapped her hands. "All glitzed up for my party, I see," she said. Mum shook her head and pointed at the wall clock.

15

"Oh no. We're going up to bed in a minute, Mrs Crumbleboom" she said. Fizzy groaned. "So unfair!" Bandit growled like he didn't think much of this idea either.

Mrs Crumbleboom looked disappointed.

"But I made so many cakes," she said.
"And all my friends will be coming."
Mum sighed. "Fine. We'll come over for
a piece of cake and to meet your friends
and then it's definitely bedtime."

Fizzy clapped her hands in delight and sprayed herself with more furniture polish.

Chapter Three

After Mum had swapped her slippers
for some trainers, they all crawled
through the hole in the fence and into
Mrs Crumbleboom's garden. Fizzy
Pop immediately skipped over to the
table on the patio which was laden with
cakes and biscuits.

"Did you bake all these?" she asked.
"Yes! I was stirring and sieving and
kneading and rolling all afternoon."
Fizzy reached for a gingerbread
man and bit off his leg. Then she
began to pick off the biscuit's
chocolate button eyes.

"Why are you having a party anyway?" Fizzy asked, her mouth open and still full of food.

"Because it's a Tuesday!" Mrs Crumbleboom said.

"A school night," Mum reminded everyone.

"Have a slice of Swiss roll," Mrs Crumbleboom said, handing Mum a plate loaded with treats. "And an iced bun. Oh, I have waffles too."

"That's very kind, Mrs Crumbleboom, but we won't stay long," Mum said firmly.

"But what about the fireworks?"
Fizzy asked.

"Yes, I've bought Roman candles and
fountains and rockets and Catherine
wheels," Mrs Crumbleboom said.

"Sounds fun but we haven't the time.
Sorry, Mrs Crumbleboom."

"Well you can't go until my band get here," Mrs Crumbleboom said, glancing at her watch.

"You're in a band?" Fizzy asked.
"Yes. It's a rock band. We call ourselves The Whippersnappers. I play drums. Mrs Strummer from Number 34 plays guitar and Mr Cackle from Number 96 sings. We're excellent."

"Cool!" Fizzy said, eyeing the table
and spotting a Bakewell tart. She
licked her lips.
"Don't even think about it," Mum said.

"Think about what?" Fizzy asked, wondering if Mum could read her mind, when a blue haired woman with a walking stick pushed open the back door and hopped onto the patio. She had a guitar slung over her shoulder.

Her jeans were ripped. Following her was an elderly man, tall, with his hair gelled up into spikes.

"Hey, Mrs Strummer! Mr Cackle!" Mrs Crumbleboom called out excitedly, rushing to the man and woman and high-fiving them.

"Can we stay and listen?" Fizzy pleaded. "Then bed. Just ten minutes."
"Two minutes," Mum suggested.
"Five," Fizzy said.

Chapter Four

Bandit barked. Mum swayed. Fizzy
danced and span and hooted.
The Whippersnappers played loudly
and the party was alive. After two
songs they stopped for a snack break.

Fizzy looked across at Mum who smiled and said, "OK. Let's go now." "We can't! I need the toilet!" Fizzy announced and, before Mum could protest, she hurtled into Mrs Crumbleboom's house and closed the back door.

Mrs Crumbleboom's house smelled of
lemons. All the pictures on the walls
were of rock stars or famous bakers.
Fizzy did actually need the loo but,
instead of being as quick as she could,

31

she took her time examining
everything: the pink toilet roll, the
little bottles of shampoos and lotions,
the stack of old newspapers and
magazines, the typewriter.

"I'm not even tired," Fizzy told herself, washing her hands and doing star jumps in front of the mirror to make sure she didn't yawn or let her eyelids go floppy. "I could stay up for hours and not even blink."

"Are you finished in there, Fizzy?"
It was Mum, knocking on the
bathroom door.
Fizzy opened the door wide, pushed
past Mum, and did a wonky cartwheel
across the carpet.

Then she began to do a jig that made her look a little bit like she was on fire. Bandit gambolled in from the garden and joined her, barking, chasing his tail, and nipping at the air excitedly. His party dress was covered in jam.

Mum put her hands on her hips. "I think we are all, not just tired, but overtired," she suggested.

"No such thing!" Fizzy announced,

spinning on the spot so fast she tumbled and Mum had to reach out to prevent her from falling against the radiator. "Let's go," Mum said. "I'll read you a story."

In the garden, The Whippersnappers
were about to begin another
tune. "Leaving already?" Mrs
Crumbleboom asked.
"Mum is making me go to bed and I
haven't even seen the fireworks,"
Fizzy said.

"That's right, I am," Mum admitted.
"Goodnight everyone! Thank you for
the cakes!"

Chapter Five

Mum closed the storybook and Fizzy said, "That was a funny story. Can you read me another one? Can you read me a scary story?"

Mum smiled. "I think what you need is a good long sleep, Fizzy Pop!"

Fizzy sat up tall in bed. "But I'm *still* not tired," she said. "I keep telling you. I'm not tired. Not even one little bit. It isn't fair. Bandit doesn't go to sleep when he's excited and wants to chew things."

Bandit, who was gnawing a teddy's arm at the end of Fizzy's bed, raised his head guiltily.

"Night, Fizzy," Mum said, kissing her forehead.

"But, Mum. I won't sleep. Why aren't you *listening*? I'm so awake I could fly a kite or eat a pancake or take a trip."

"Take a trip where?" Mum asked.
"Anywhere," Fizzy said.
"Tell me... Are you awake enough to go camping?" Mum asked.
"Yes!" Fizzy said. "I am so awake; look into my eyeballs!"

She opened her eyes very wide and
stared at Mum.
Mum rubbed her chin and thought
carefully for a minute. "OK. Wait here."

Chapter Six

After a few minutes, Mum returned with a dining chair. While Fizzy watched, Mum pulled the duvet over the chair to make space beneath it on the floor.

She found a blanket from Fizzy's wardrobe and laid it carefully along the space, adding a pillow from the bed. Then she turned off the bedroom light and opened the curtains. Finally, she crawled into the space. "Come on Fizzy. Let's camp ourselves to sleep!"

Fizzy giggled and crept in next to
Mum. Bandit followed. And together
they all closed their eyes.

Suddenly they heard a bang.
"It's a robber!" Fizzy said. And then
another bang. And then a whizz.

And then, through the window, lights
in the sky. Huge explosions of colour.
Fizzy couldn't believe her luck.
"The fireworks!"
"The fireworks," Mummy repeated.
"Can we go outside and look at them?
Just for five minutes?"

Mum smiled and wrapped her arm around Fizzy. "Not a chance," she said.